A business consultant ╎ ╟╟╟╢╢ ╟╟╢╢ ╷veil recounts his childhood memories of ╎ ╨ts and grandparents – through the use of characters who represent many of his friend's children that have now also become friends with children of their own. He places great value on all family and friends and the joy of being a grandparent and parent.

To all my friends and family, who have shared a lifetime full of fun and friendship.

A special thanks to my wife, Sharon, who shared the adventure from the initial finding of a "lost" golf ball whilst out walking in Spain. My sister-in-law, Christine, who provided her constructive editing skills and, Liam, who listened to my ideas and ramblings over several weeks of walks in the Cheshire countryside.

Grandpa and Phoebe's Amazing Adventures

Synopsis

The lost golf triplets

This is an adventure story about a young girl, Phoebe Shortshanks, and her very unusual grandparents.

Join Phoebe as she works with Grandpa on some of his amazing, but sometimes disastrous, magical inventions on a journey of discovery and friendship.

Who can believe that animals can talk and be so organised as to help a lost golf ball be reunited with her lost brothers?

Phoebe, along with her animal friends organises a daring rescue to release a lost and lonely golf ball, Putty, from the evil driving range.

To do this, they will have to rely on Grandpa's magical inventions and the determination of Phoebe and all her animal friends.

From Lymm to La Manga the excitement is gripping.

Chapter 1
Aged 8 and 2/3rds
Going on 40!

"Grandpa will you take me with you to play golf please, pretty please?" begged Phoebe.

Phoebe loved her grandparents, Grandpa and Grandma Shortshanks, and always looked forward to her weekends when she got to stay at the "crooked house, with the crooked shed and twisted people." Well that was always what Mummy called her grandparents' house. "And keep out of that dreadful crooked dirty old shed, it's dangerous," said Mummy Brodrick Shortshanks, who had refused to fully adopt her husband's name as Shortshanks had a "dreadful ring to it."

Saturday was ''BIG SHOP DAY' and it was important, said Mummy, that someone who is clumsy and always runs everywhere before bumping into something, falling over and shouting "ow!"!" is kept well away from the supermarkets to avoid a national disaster especially after your last visit!

Phoebe really didn't mind as she found shopping boring unless you could take your saxophone and give it a long loud blast behind some poor unsuspecting shopper who then dropped a large bottle of gravy browning all over the floor, creating the most disgusting mess that caused an enormous lady to deliberately slip over and shout "where's there's blame there's a claim" and then a small boy to attempt to slide through the gravy on one leg before landing headfirst in between the chocolates and the biscuits. "Surely the shelves should have been able to withstand the impact of a four-year-old boy," said Daddy Shortshanks as he protested Phoebe's innocence to the gathering crowd of onlookers, store detectives, and first aiders, who continued to spread the gravy browning into aisles 6, 7and 8, making the entire area look like a scene from the decapitation of Henry the eighth, or was it one of his wives?

"If you are going to speak to us in that tone of voice we shall take our custom elsewhere," said Daddy to the extremely angry store manager, who looked like his red face was about to burst, "Phoebe is a very talented saxophone player and her playing has nothing to do with the careless actions and poor layout of your store which caused this dreadful mess," protested Daddy grabbing Phoebe's arm, and along with Mummy, made a sharp exit abandoning the "big shop trolley" in the big hole, that had been created by the small boy, between aisles 5 and 6, as he crashed through the chocolates and biscuits. It was amazing how a full bar of chocolate had landed in his mouth!

As Phoebe left the store being dragged through the door by Daddy firmly holding on to her left hand, and tightly holding onto her saxophone in her right, she looked back to survey the carnage left behind. She was particularly impressed with the swirling brown patterns the shopping trolley had created, but perhaps even more impressive was the speed at which Mummy had got into the car and was revving the engine shouting, "Get in, get in,", followed by "let's go, let's go!!!" Mummy always said things twice when she meant something was really, really, real!

Mummy Brodrick Shortshanks was hopping mad, as she drove like Lewis Hamilton through the supermarket car park successfully negotiating a trolley boy, who managed to clear a four feet barrier to avoid being run over. Once clear of the supermarket Mummy started to calm down a bit and recount the circumstances that had caused their departure.

"Why did you have to give such a blast on your saxophone just as that poor big fat lady was trying to reach for the brown sauce and gravy browning?" asked Mummy.

"Well," started Phoebe, "I knew she couldn't reach unless she really stretched for it, and I thought that a loud blast of C sharp would produce the desired musical therapy that would create the extra 2cm of stretch required."

Phoebe was renowned for her powerful arguments or was it that she couldn't be wrong! Daddy said she was a "stubborn but proud ginger who found it impossible to admit to mistakes."

"That's not true, Daddy," screamed Phoebe, "I am not ginger I am auburn!!!"

Phoebe muttered to herself, "Why was it that adults always seemed to think that children were not as clever as them, and always thought adults knew best.". This was simply not true. After all, this fiercely proud stubborn ginger was always correcting Mummy and Daddy when they were wrong!!!

Meanwhile, Mummy had arrived to drop Phoebe at the "crooked house with the twisted people", better known as Grandmas and Grandpas. This was a welcome break from the arguing as Daddy declared that Phoebe might only be 8 and 2/3rds but she was going on 40!

Phoebe ran up the path to find Grandma and Grandpa only to be greeted by Swish the dog, a whirling dervish of a scruffy mutt who was always hungry and had the awful habit of making the most horrible silent but deadly farts (SBDs) at the most inappropriate time. This always made Phoebe laugh as Grandma was always blaming Grandpa for the strange smells!

"Tell Grandpa why we have to go to that awful supermarket, Diddle, now," said Daddy shouting out of the passenger side window of the car as it sped off jolting and backfiring. "See you in an hour or so and keep out of trouble" was the last thing Phoebe heard from Daddy as the car disappeared at great speed.

Phoebe turned to see that Grandpa was just leaving to play golf and Grandma and Swish the Dog was shouting instructions after him as to what time he had to be home for his tea. That's obviously Grandma shouting the instructions because obviously, dogs can't speak, can they?

Chapter 2
Interesting Times at Grandpa's and Grandma's

Visiting Grandma's and Grandpa's house was always exciting and something that Phoebe always looked forward to. "Is Grandpa a magician or just a brilliant inventor?" she asked Daddy. "And why does Grandma never seem to like any of his inventions?" He didn't answer out loud but just smiled knowingly back at Phoebe, as he had long ago ceased to be amazed at how his father could create so much havoc so easily, and how his mother seemed to be constantly telling him off or clearing up after his latest disaster.

Grandma was a wonderful, kind, and gentle woman, but she always seemed to be on Grandpa's case irrespective of what task or kind deed he was trying to complete for her. They loved each other very much but they always seemed to be bickering over the slightest thing. Grandpa was always in the "doghouse"" as he called it. Phoebe had asked Daddy to explain what this meant as she thought that Grandma had made him move into Swish the Dog's basket under the kitchen table!

This was just one of many strange expressions that Grandpa constantly used. Mummy said not to listen as he was "barking mad". This made no sense at all to Phoebe and she became even more confused when Daddy explained that Grandma was "much worse than her bite". This was particularly frightening as Phoebe didn't even know that she did bite! Not even Swish the dog would bite you, even if you grabbed his tail, which he was always chasing around and around in circles, and why Grandma regularly shouted at him calling him "a stupid mutt without a brain that made a better floor mop than a dog".

Grandma was only 1.5m tall but made up for that by also being 1.5m wide. She had grey curly hair and always wore the rimmed spectacles that she bought just after the Second World War had finished saying they would "see her out". Her ample bosom was always covered by a 'Grandma' cardigan, unless she was baking, in which case the cardigan had to be hung on the back of the kitchen chair to enable the full force of Grandma's not insignificant wobbly arms to flap around causing the scone mixture to surrender quickly, with the clouds of flour adding to Grandma's already very grey hair. She may be small, but Grandma had the most enormous heart and would do anything for Phoebe.

In many ways Grandpa was the opposite of Grandma, as he was very tall and slim with long thin fingers, that were always busy making another magic invention in his crooked shed at the end of the garden. Grandpa was always losing his glasses, but usually, he had forgotten that they were on top of his head. There was nothing more that Grandpa liked than trying to invent a new "labour-saving gadget that would revolutionise the world". Most of these ended in disaster.

Take the automatic pancake tosser that he had made for Grandma on her birthday last year, which by chance happened to be on Pancake Tuesday.

Grandma had unwrapped the curious Birthday parcel to discover what was her favourite frying pan, with various wires and attachments connected to it. It was now so huge that it took up all the rings on the cooker. Despite her protests, Grandpa convinced her that it was worth "this small inconvenience" and "to just try it," he said with a proud smile on his face. Grandma set to work, removing her cardigan and placing it on the back of the kitchen chair exposing her full wobbly arms that were about to take on the arduous task of making the "lightest pancake mixture possible".".

Swish the dog sensed that something magical, or possibly disastrous, was about to happen. Why wouldn't it? Grandpa was looking very pleased, almost smug, and stood in the kitchen connecting his latest invention whilst Grandma was busy mixing jam and cream, both of which were Swish's favourites in equal measures. It was time for him to get out of his basket and be ready to lick up any falling drops of the delicious pancake mixture, that would surely be the result of Grandma's wobbly arms and flapping muscles reaching full power. Swish knew he had to be careful and quick, as Grandma was just as likely to kick him up the bum as she was to start shouting at Grandpa, should either of them get in the way or disturb her increasing concentration.

As the auto tosser sprung into life, Grandpa explained to Grandma that "all you need to do is pour the mixture in the pan and stand back and watch as the auto tosser detects when the pancake is perfectly cooked. It then scoops up the jam and cream, adding it to the centre of the pancake, before tossing it high into the air sealing the jam and cream into the centre." Grandma suddenly looked horrified. She always referred to Grandpa by his first name Gordon however, according to how much trouble he was in accorded the length to which she would scream and extend his name. Grandma had realised that Grandpa, Gordon, (his real name but only ever used if Phoebe needed to introduce Grandpa to any of her friends) knew nothing about cooking and that no one EVER put the cream and jam into a pancake until AFTER it had been tossed!!!

"GOOOOOOOOOOOOOORRRRRRRDONNNNNNNN N!!!" screamed Grandma, but it was too late the pancake tosser had already scooped up the jam and added it to the centre of the pancake and was now returning to add the cream with a great dollop and splosh. Swish the Dog looked on in anticipation as the pancake was hurled high into the air, over Grandpa's and Grandma's shoulders, before getting stuck on the ceiling, half covering the light, and dropping its contents all over Grandma and the floor. Swish pounced onto the jam and cream dripping down Grandma's glasses onto the floor and immediately licked it up as if this would be the last piece of food he ever had. He need not have worried!

"GOOOOOOOOOOOOORRRRRRRRRRRRDDDDDD DOOOOOONNNNNNNNNNN, turn the pesky thing off," bellowed Grandma. Too late! The auto tosser was in full flow now and had refilled with a new round of mixture, and was just completing the jam and cream run, as Grandpa was trying to find the 'off' switch. "I knew I should have used a bigger button," said Grandpa who was now frantically trying to find the very small 'off' button, but this is impossible when your glasses are on top of your head!

The auto tosser launched another missile, narrowly missing Grandma but making a perfect hit on the back door, creating a particularly nice red and white jam and cream pattern that was slowly sliding down the door to the floor. Swish saw this as a great chance to practise his acrobatic skills, as he leapt to lick the jam from the highest point on the door. This was also very good for improving the pattern. Swish looked amazing as he now had jam and cream all over his ears and tail, as well as large chunks of pancake stuck to his tummy.

After "firing" 14 rounds of pancakes, jam, and cream all over the kitchen, the auto tosser finally came to a halt just as Grandpa found his glasses and Grandma found her favourite frying pan which had become detached and miraculously was in her hands as she gave Grandpa an unceremonious whack on the bottom, as he ran for the safety of the shed. Swish decided Grandpa was not as daft as he looked, and the shed seemed to be the safest place for him too. "Just wait till I get my hands on you and that useless mutt of a dog" Grandma yelled, as they both fled from the kitchen. The mess was horrendous, but this was nothing compared to the danger of a pancake-covered Grandma armed with a frying pan!

That was three weeks ago, and Grandpa had managed to clean most of the mess up, but Swish kept finding the odd piece of pancake as it dropped from the ceiling complete with a crunchy bit of jam and cream still clinging on to it.

Phoebe was not sure if Grandma and Grandpa were friends again yet, though she had noticed that Grandpa was now only "Gooorddon", so things must be improving!

Chapter 3
The Magic of the Golf Course

"Please Grandpa you promised me that you would take me with you next time you went to play, please, please, please," begged Phoebe, looking at Grandpa with her gorgeous green eyes poking out from beneath her favourite baseball cap that splayed her "auburn" (ginger and proud hair!) around her angelic face. Phoebe was an expert negotiator, especially when it came to be having her own way with Grandpa.

"Oh, Pheebs, you are so persuasive. How can an old Grandpa like me refuse you anything?" said Grandpa. "I tell you what, you can be my caddy."

"What's a caddy?" asked Phoebe, confident that she had won the argument with Grandpa and he had finally agreed to take her with him to play golf.

"Well," said Grandpa, "you get to carry my golf clubs and make sure I have the correct club to play my next shot wherever we are on the course."

"But Grandpa how will I know which of your club thingamajigs you need, and when? There are lots of them in your golf bag and it looks far too heavy for me to carry," pleaded Phoebe with a knowing smile deliberately thrown to be caught by Grandpa's kind heart.

"Don't worry, Pheebs, you can use my electric trolley and I will show you which buttons make it go forward and backwards on its own, so you just have to guide it. I'll explain which golf clubs—not thingamajigs—I need to play the shot and if you are really good, I will even let you have a go," said Grandpa.

"OOOO Grandpa you are the best person in the whole wide world," squealed Phoebe in delight, as this confirmed her negotiation skills were still first class.

As quick as a flash Grandpa had loaded the electric trolley and all the thingamajig golf stick things into the bright red Morris Minor, that Phoebe always thought looked like one of Grandma's jelly and blancmange puddings, wibbling and wobbling on a plate. "We're off to the golf club for a jolly good swish and a curse," cried Grandpa as they sped away.

The golf club was reached by a long winding road, that looked quite sinister to Phoebe at first, but once they rounded the last bend, they turned into something that seemed like a magic enchanted park. It was full of beautiful trees and undulating green strips of grass separated by lots of sandpits with some very strange-looking castles with flags flying on what looked like upturned green hats. "What do you think Pheebs?" asked Grandpa. "Oh, Grandpa it's wonderful, I have never seen such a beautiful garden. Look there's a squirrel," pointed Phoebe, and "wow, wow, wow is that a badger Grandpa?" yelled Phoebe as she swivelled her favourite baseball cap to face backwards so she could get a better look.

"Calm down Pheebs we have not even parked the car yet"," said Grandpa. "I need you to get all of my clubs out of the car and onto the trolley then we can go over to the first tee and get started. Remember Pheebs no running, shouting, and definitely no playing your saxophone! Just one last thing Pheebs."

"What Grandpa?" enquired Phoebe with her best-knowing smile, thinking that another negotiation was just about to start. "Well," said Grandpa in a very hesitant voice, "you know I love playing golf?"

"Of course, I do," said Phoebe, "why did you ask me that Grandpa?"

"Um, it's probably nothing but I also enjoy a…" Grandpa hesitated as if he was about to jump into a very cold swimming pool, and then with a final gush he blurted out,

"...A...flipping good curse whilst I'm playing. So, promise me if you hear anything you shouldn't, you won't grass me up to Grandma," with an expression on his face that suggested a great crime was about to be committed and Phoebe was the prime witness for the prosecution, namely Grandma!

Grandpa explained that cursing was not anywhere near as bad as swearing. He felt he was merely encouraging his golf balls to go in the direction he wanted. "Don't worry, Grandpa, Mummy always says I have selective hearing when I want to, so I will just pretend not to hear."

Grandpa explained how the strange-looking device on wheels was an electric golf trolley that carried the golf clubs. "It takes the weight off my old bones: let me show you how it works," said Grandpa as he demonstrated what each button did. Phoebe loved it, thinking it was very upright and rather jolly, just like a large toy soldier. Phoebe experimented pressing the various buttons but the best button of all was the one that made the newly named "Jolly Trolley" march off on its own when she pressed it. The golf thingamajig sticks looked like they were a gaggle of geese running away from Farmer Phoebe, but like magic, after just 10 metres they all obediently stopped to wait for their next instruction. Grandpa tittered as he watched Phoebe trying to master the various controls and at how easily she had created a new friend in the "Jolly Trolley".

Grandpa introduced Phoebe to a very nice chap with a funny moustache that almost touched his ears when he spoke. "This is Mr T Starter, a very good friend of mine. He makes sure everything around here runs like clockwork," said Grandpa. "Good morning little boy," said Mr T, "you look just like your grandpa. Are you here to play golf or the saxophone? By the way, your hat's on back to front."

"I am not a little boy," said a very disgruntled Phoebe. "This is my favourite hat that I deliberately turned backwards, so I could get a better look at the badger I just saw over there, and I never go anywhere without my saxophone because…" replied a hesitant Phoebe trying to think of a really good answer to Mr T's questions.

"Oh, I see," interrupted Mr T, "well that makes perfect sense and is very sensible indeed. By the way, the badger you saw is Old Bobby Badger. He lives over by the sixth hole, the one that backs onto the wood, and he is always with his girlfriend Nel the Squirrel (she's French you know). Enjoy your game and keep out of trouble," he said to Grandpa as he patted Phoebe on the head causing her cap to spin.

"Why does everyone tell me to keep out of trouble?" protested Phoebe.

"Don't worry about Mr T, he is quite potty, he has names for all the animals on the course and even claims that they talk to him. Crazy! He just means that we should try to play well, so come on let's get going," laughed Grandpa. Interesting, thought Phoebe, as she straightened her cap, adjusted her saxophone, and handed Grandpa the thingamajig stick called Mr Driver!!!

Swoosh, Swish…woosh, PING……………thud, bounce, bounce roll.

"WOW,", squealed Phoebe, "that WAS FANTASTIC Grandpa it has gone miles and miles and landed just over there by that huge tree."

"Thanks, Pheebs. I'm glad you could see it, my eyes are not as good as they used to be, even when I remember to put my glasses on," laughed Grandpa as he took his glasses off the top of his head and positioned them over his eyes after he had hit the golf ball!

Phoebe and Grandpa set off down the middle of the green stripy bit, past the sandy beachy bits and up to the tree where Grandpa's ball had landed. Phoebe concentrated ever so hard to make sure that the Jolly Trolley stayed just in front of them as they happily walked hand in hand down what Grandpa said was a fairway. Phoebe thought that this was an under-estimation, and it should be called an "excitement way". Grandpa agreed that she was right and wished he could capture this wonderful precious moment with his Granddaughter and "bottle it as it could save the world."

As Grandpa and Phoebe walked down the green carpet towards the beautiful old tree, that stood tall and proud surveying all before it, Phoebe noticed that Grandpa was becoming quite agitated and was sure that one of his cursing episodes was about to start!

"Beejeebers!"!" cried Grandpa, "That tree has had it in for me, ever since last summer. It hides my golf balls under its roots every time I play this hole," said Grandpa.

When they arrived at the huge old tree, Phoebe noticed the roots were growing out of the ground in all directions and stretched towards you like Grandpa's fingers, when he handed you a biscuit.

"Do you recognise anything familiar about it?" asked Grandpa. "Look closer and tell me if it reminds you of anything in Grandma's kitchen."

Phoebe studied the old tree, which though gnarled and weather-beaten, had a very regal, almost stubborn air about it, probably because of the many winter storms it had lived through. Grandpa said that the tree was even older than him and that the "great lump of firewood was in the wrong place, but it deserved to see out its days looking out over the golf course. I just hope it's not too long now!" added Grandpa as he searched in vain for his ball. Phoebe noticed that it was hidden under one of the roots and she had to use all her eight-and-two-thirds-year-old strength to release the ball. Phoebe could have sworn, (well no she wouldn't swear…she would have to leave that to Grandpa!), that the tree was holding onto the golf ball and that the root seemed to be stroking her hand!

"I found it," cried Phoebe to Grandpa who was off round the other side cursing the old tree whilst searching for his lost ball.

"Do you recognise it yet Pheebs?" said Grandpa pointing to part of the tree's roots." Look it's where I took the piece of root from, that I used to repair Grandma's kitchen table," laughed Grandpa. Phoebe remembered how last summer Grandma's kitchen table had a terribly wonky set of legs that made it impossible to eat your fish, chips, and curry from the Chinese chippy down the road, without spilling it all into your lap. Grandma wanted to get a "modern table with a nice fold-out leaf, like they had on the TV" but Grandpa had insisted that they were too expensive and that it would not go with the rest of the kitchen. "All that was needed was a temporary repair that would blend in," he argued. Grandpa had created a small adjustable fifth leg. What Grandpa hadn't realised was that the root from the old tree was still alive and well and had taken control of the entire table. The living root had the ability to raise, lower, shake or even extend its leg, especially to trip Swish the dog as he tried to get in or out of his basket that was kept under the table!

There had been several strange incidents over the last year or so with the kitchen table behaving very mischievously. Grandma said it was a dear old table but possessed. Grandpa had laughed and said, "it was not dear, it was a Fiver!" This was quite clearly one of Grandpa's jokes that he thought was hilarious, but nobody else got it. "The table with five legs! Do you get it Pheebs?" laughed Grandpa.

Grandpa regularly made a joke about Swish the dog "being under a fiver" every time he went into his basket. This was followed by one of Swish's SBDs which suggested that Swish did not appreciate Grandpa's jokes either. Swish was always very dubious when going anywhere near Fiver as he knew that the table would play a trick on him when he was not looking.

With the various explanations of how Fiver had been created from part of the old tree roots and Grandpa's ball having been found by Phoebe, Grandpa was finally ready to continue with his game.

"On we go Pheebs" SWISH, SWISH, SWOSH, and Grandpa's ball was off sailing down the "excitement way".

Jolly Trolley Soldier

controls

Chapter 4
I Can't Find My Ball Anywhere.
Where Do They All Go?

As Grandpa and Phoebe continued their exciting round of golf, Grandpa's ball had already visited the "beach" (that's what Grandpa called the sandy bits),), and then with a mighty swish from thingamajig sandy stick, Grandpa's ball flew from the "beach" high into the blue sky, missing the upturned green hat with the flag-waving peacefully in the wind, and landed in the Enchanted Wood at the back of the sixth green, where Bobby the Badger and Nel the Squirrel lived.

"Blood and stomach pills, where has that gone," shouted Grandpa. "Oh dear, Grandpa," said Phoebe, "have you got a poorly tummy, and have you cut your finger? Let me have a look." Just then Phoebe pressed the button on the "Jolly Trolley" by accident and didn't even notice it march forward towards and over the embankment into the Enchanted Wood. "Sorry Phoebe," grumbled Grandpa, I am just so frustrated when the ball doesn't go where it's supposed to."

"Oh," replied Phoebe, "I didn't realise you were CURSING, but don't worry I saw the ball bounce just into the wood: it will be easy to find."

"Hmmm, that's what you think!" replied Grandpa as he suddenly heard a loud bang followed by the clatter of golf thingamajigs crashing down the steep embankment that was the edge of the wooden corpse that Grandpa called the Enchanted Wood. "OOPS," said Phoebe, "I thought I had turned the Jolly Trolley off Grandpa. It must have a fault with its electrical thingies or perhaps it has a mind of its own?"

"Don't worry. Pheebs," replied Grandpa, "it's my ruddy discombobulated golf balls that have a mind of their own. Sometimes they are evil little things, always getting into trouble and disappearing without a trace."

"Oh, Grandpa you do exaggerate, and stop cursing!" cautioned Phoebe, "Come on let's go and get the Jolly Trolley and the thingamajigs back, and we might even find your golf ball. Mind your step on this embankment it's a bit slippy." Phoebe held out her hand to Grandpa, which he grasped just as her feet left the grassy slope and she landed on her bottom and started to career down like a sledge cutting through snow, only the sledge was Grandpa, and the snow was thick mud!

"Whoa," screamed Phoebe. Quickly gathering speed, they slid down the embankment, through the nettle patch, past Bobby the Badger's sett, before Grandpa came to rest landing feet first in the stream. Phoebe had managed to wrap her feet up around Grandpa's knees as she experienced quite an exciting sleigh ride, avoiding most of the mud and nettles, unlike Grandpa who was covered in it and even had clumps of grass sticking out of his not inconsiderably large ears!

Everything had changed so quickly. The bright green stripes and upturned hats with waving flags had been replaced with twisted tree stumps covered in magical twinkling mosses, black, thick smelly mud, large overgrown thorny bushes, scattered golf thingamajig sticks, and golf balls everywhere. Phoebe was still sitting on Grandpa, admiring the new view. As she looked around, she noticed Percy the Pigeon high up in the twisted tree who appeared to be laughing, as were Nel the Squirrel and Bobby the Badger. This was a truly strange place, with completely different sounds and animals, who Phoebe was sure were talking to each other and laughing at her and Grandpa's predicament.

"Phoebe darling are you OK?" asked a very worried Grandpa as he pulled the clumps of grass from his ears and desperately searched for his glasses, which had miraculously survived the sleigh ride and were still on top of his head!

Phoebe and Grandpa got to their feet slowly and carefully, walked the few steps to where the Jolly Trolley had come to a stop in the stream, lying on its side, with the contents scattered all around. Very slowly and carefully Phoebe and Grandpa started to gather all the golf thingamajig sticks and place them back in the Jolly Trolley. Grandpa was using his extra-long fingers to fiddle with the electrical "doodah" when suddenly the Jolly Trolley jumped back to life, albeit looking like it was badly in need of a trip to the car wash! With a sudden whirring and clinking sound, the Jolly Trolley started to climb out of the wood, heading back to the peaceful green stripes and waving flags.

Phoebe and Grandpa were now scrambling around in the mud looking for Grandpa's golf ball. Phoebe was now starting to agree with Grandpa, that perhaps they did have a mind of their own. Suddenly Phoebe noticed a small mole with huge round eyes, watching her from the mound of twinkling moss. "Hello," said Phoebe "what's your name?" Then came the most amazing response. In the quietest, smallest voice Phoebe had ever heard the tiny creature answered, "Millie."

"You can speak!!!" shrieked Phoebe.

"Of course, I can speak! How else do you think we all communicate with each other in this beautiful wood that is our home? Bobby Badger, come here, and you too Percy Pigeon. Stop laughing from up there on your high perch and meet our new friends who have paid us a surprise visit, even if they weren't invited!"

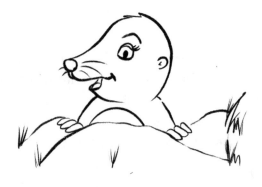

"Oh, I'm so sorry that we arrived unannounced," replied Phoebe, but we were looking for Grandpa's golf ball. I'm afraid it has a bit of a mind of its own. Grandpa certainly didn't ask it to come over here, he wanted it to be next to the waving flag on the upturned hat thing up there," pointing to the other side of the wood.

"Phoebe where are you?" shouted Grandpa, who was now clambering up the embankment after the Jolly Trolley, which had successfully navigated the slope and was standing to attention by the side of the waving flag, waiting for its next order. "I'm coming Grandpa," replied Phoebe as she turned to reluctantly say goodbye to her group of new friends. "I have to go as Grandpa will be looking for me and worrying, or else he might just forget that I am with him. If he goes home without me Grandma will definitely kill him, possibly twice, once for the state of his clothes and secondly for leaving me behind. Can I come back another time?" asked Phoebe. In a rather deep, gruff voice Bobby the Badger said, "you can come back but only if you promise not to slide through my front garden outside my sett. That's my house you know!"

"Oops, I'm so sorry, but it was an accident," apologised Phoebe. "Dooo youuuu want this before you gooo," cooed Percy Pigeon. Phoebe looked closely at what appeared to be a lump of mud held tightly in Percy Pigeon's beak. Percy dropped it, so it landed at Phoebe's feet. "Oh, thank you so much," said Phoebe as she realised that beneath the mud was Grandpa's golf ball, the one "with a mind of its own!" As she quickly pushed it deep into her coat pocket, Phoebe was sure that she could hear muffled voices as she clambered back up the embankment, shouting goodbye to her new friends as she went.

"Eh up Pheebs there's hardly a mark on you and look at me! Grandma's going to go mad, well even madder than she already is! I think it's time we got home, and I will try and clean myself up in the shed before she spots me, or else I'm dickery done for," said Grandpa.

"What an adventure we had Grandpa, and we met all those new friends," said Phoebe in her cheery and excited way." They were all so nice, particularly Millie Mole and Percy Pigeon who chatted away with me, and then found your golf ball," said Phoebe. This was greeted by an unconvincing "Ugh?" from Grandpa adding, "You really do have a vivid imagination. Are you sure you didn't bang your head on a branch when we slid down the muddy bank?" asked Grandpa. "You will be telling me next that golf balls can talk too, and that they really do have a mind of their own. I suppose they don't get lost but just disappear into a magical golf ball world. Perhaps that's where all the golf balls go," laughed Grandpa.

Phoebe began to wonder if she had imagined it as she and Grandpa, accompanied by Jolly Trolley, made their way back to the car for the journey home and the task of trying to get everyone and everything clean before Grandma found out. What were those muffled noises and vibrations coming from Phoebe's very muddy pocket?

Chapter 5
The Shrinkability Cupboard

Swish the dog was snoozing in his basket under Fiver the table when he was rudely awakened by the unmistakeable sound of Grandpa's car backfiring, as it came to a halt in the drive.

Grandpa and Phoebe headed straight to the crooked shed with all their messy gear, especially the Jolly Trolley. Grandpa decided to bob his head around the kitchen door and let Grandma know they were home, but as luck would have it, she had popped next door to see Mrs Bridges for a cup of tea and a piece of cake.

Mrs Bridges was from Scotland and always insisted on giving Phoebe a big sloppy kiss whenever she saw her and called everything "Wee". For a while, Phoebe thought she was always getting caught short and was obsessed with going to the loo, but apparently "wee" means small in Scotland.

There was a note, by the kettle, from Grandma, explaining that she had just "nipped out and would be back in about an hour". Grandpa knew that once Grandma and Mrs Bridges got together for a cup of tea it always resulted in a "jolly good chinwag" accompanied by lots of cake and "a wee drop of sherry".

Grandpa said that sometimes Grandma came back "quite squiffy", but Grandma always said she was not squiffy and had only had a small "drinkie drink" just to keep Mrs Bridges company.

"We're in luck Pheebs," cheered Grandpa, "we've got the kitchen to ourselves. Go and get the Jolly Trolley and I'll show you my latest labour-saving invention, the Shrinkability Cupboard." Phoebe ran to the shed and quickly returned with the very muddy Jolly Trolley. She was brimming with excitement to see what Grandpa's latest invention was going to do.

"What does the Shrinkability Cupboard do Grandpa? How does it work?" cried Phoebe bursting with anticipation.

"Well," said Grandpa, "Grandma wanted me to make the kitchen bigger because she said she needs more space to store all the things she is always making. But I thought extending the kitchen was going to be too expensive so why didn't I just make a cupboard that would shrink anything that was put into it! Clever eh Pheebs?"

"But once you have made something smaller how do you get it to come back to normal size? How does it all work Grandpa?" asked Phoebe.

"It's just simple molecular physics Pheebs. We just rearrange all the molecules and compress them down into a more efficient space. So, if we put the Jolly Trolley into the Shrinkability Cupboard we can set the dial to very small and shrink it down, so it will fit into the palm of my hand. Then we can simply rinse it under the tap, get rid of the mud, bring it back to its normal size and it will be all shiny and clean and we have not had to do any hard work," said a very enthusiastic Grandpa.

"OK, Grandpa, but how do we get it back to its original size, or else the Jolly Trolley will be no good for us to play golf with again?" demanded Phoebe.

"That's a little more difficult," said Grandpa, "there are only two ways to restore the original molecular structure. The first is to set off a vibration that shakes everything back into place, but to do this you need something like a musical instrument that can replicate the sounds and vibrations of when the shrinking took place. The second is to reset the dial to large but I'm afraid I have not perfected that yet, but I'm' working on it Pheebs."

With that, Grandpa heaved the Jolly Trolley into the Shrinkability Cupboard, turned the dial, and said to Phoebe, "Quickly play a piece of music that we can then use to reverse the molecular deconstruction later." As quick as a molecular deconstruction flash Phoebe grabbed her saxophone and started to play one of her favourite tunes, Three Blind Mice. There was an incredible crashing and banging from the cupboard and Grandpa had to hold it shut with his shoulder. Phoebe played on, never missing a note, and just as she got to the part where the farmer's wife gets the carving knife, everything went quiet, and the cupboard stopped jumping around. Grandpa shouted, "OK, all done Pheebs!" The silence and anticipation were incredible as Grandpa slowly opened the Shrinkability Cupboard and they peered around the door into what looked like space, but there in the corner was the tiniest miniature Jolly Trolley. Grandpa picked it up using his two very long fingers, delicately carrying it to the sink." Right, Pheebs very carefully turn the tap on slowly so we can rinse all the mud off." Phoebe turned the tap to no more than a trickle and watched as the water washed the tiny amounts of mud off the miniature Jolly Trolley and into the sink.

THE SHRINKABILITY CUPBOARD

"OK Pheebs get ready," said Grandpa as he placed the miniature Jolly Trolley back onto the exact same spot in the corner of the Shrinkability Cupboard and closed the door. "Play your saxophone now but make sure it's the same molecular vibration construction as the deconstruction."

"Ugh," said Phoebe, "what on earth does that mean Grandpa?"

"Three Blind Mice," said Grandpa.

Phoebe blew her saxophone, making sure that the notes were perfect, and she never missed a beat. Just as she played the farmer's wife bit, the cupboard made a funny burping noise and the door flew open to reveal a full-sized shiny mud-free Jolly Trolley, complete with all the thingamajig golf sticky things.

"Grandpa it worked; you really have made a labour-saving device. It would have taken us hours to clean it if it was full size, instead, it took just seconds! Oh, Grandpa, you're a genius!"!" cried Phoebe.

Just then Grandma walked in looking slightly "squiffy", possibly having had a "drinkie drink", and let out the almightiest scream.

"Goooooooooooorrrrrrrrrrrrrrrrrrrddoooooooooooooooooo ooon, (positively incandescent with rage) what have you done to my sink? Why has it got bucket loads of mud in it?"

"Oops," said Grandpa, "I think I need to make a couple of adjustments to the molecular deconstruction settings Pheebs" as he ran out of the kitchen chased by Grandma and her swinging handbag, up the crooked path to the crooked shed!

Phoebe couldn't help laughing to herself as she watched the comical scene between her grandparents. "Who would have thought they were the grown-ups?" she tittered. Just then she heard a tiny voice shouting "get me out of here." It was coming from her pocket. Phoebe took out a mud-covered golf ball, took it to the muddy sink, and very gently cleaned it. She was amazed to see a shiny smiling golf ball with a beautifully shaped number 2 nose and a ruddy complexion. But even more amazing was when the golf ball started to speak!

"Hello, I'm Slice," said the golf ball.

Chapter 6
The Great Bouncing
Adventures of the Lost Balls

The sunshine beamed brightly through Grandma's kitchen window on what was turning out to be a truly wonderful day.

Goodness gracious me what a day I'm having, thought Phoebe. First the animals were talking to me and now this lovely looking golf ball is too. "Am I going mad?" Phoebe muttered to herself.

"Phoebe, if I may call you that," said Slice, the very polite golf ball, "you're not going mad, indeed you are super-duper intelligent and that is why we have selected you to help us on what is a vitally important mission. I obtained special permission from all the members of the Enchanted Wood, its council, and all the lost golf balls to be able to speak to you."

"Do you mean the animals, Bobby the Badger, Percy Pigeon, Nel the Squirrel, and Millie Mole that I met earlier when the Jolly Trolley marched off into the Enchanted Wood?" asked Phoebe, very slowly and deliberately.

"Oh, they are just some of my friends, and you've already made a very favourable impression on them with your kindness and gentleness when you helped your Dear Sweet Grandpa Gordon Shortshanks," replied Slice.

"There are many more that you still have to meet especially Freddie Fox, head of The Animal Council, and his assistant Hare Henry."

"Oh! is Herr Henry German?" asked Phoebe.

"No," replied a laughing Slice, "he's a very bouncy Moon Gazing Hare. He is always gazing at the stars and the moon and chatting with them. They tell him about things that will happen in the future. He observes everything and reports back to the Leader of the Council, Freddie Fox. Freddie is the wisest, animal, thing, or person you will ever meet. He knows everything and has agreed, that my mission is so important, that he has fully sanctioned the operation and given me permission to talk to you and ask for your help. The last time animals, things, and humans spoke to each other the great oak tree was just a baby acorn, so I think that is about 500, in what human people call years."

"But why me and how do you know my grandpa's name?" asked Phoebe. "What is so important that animals and golf balls are talking to me? Grandpa already thinks I have an even bigger imagination than…?" Phoebe was thinking of something very large but regrettably all she could come up with was "Grandma's tummy!"!"

Slice laughed out loud at such a ridiculous proclamation, which made Phoebe blush. "Your Grandma is not that big, although the size of her love for you is enormous, so perhaps that would be a better comparison?"

"You're right Slice, I just sometimes get a little clumsy with my words, as well as my feet! Grandma's bark is worse than her bite you know", still not fully understanding Grandpa's explanation of a few days ago." Phoebe replied a little embarrassed that she had been unkind about Grandma's tummy, "How do you know my grandpa and grandma anyway?" she said quickly changing the subject.

Slice continued, "We, that is all the lost golf balls, the animal council and the Enchanted Wood have been monitoring the golf club very carefully over the many moons that have risen and set over the wood. Hare Henry, in particular, is watching out for people who we feel are kind and look after our home, living peacefully and in harmony with all the trees, plants, animals, and all things in nature," said Slice. "Your Grandpa is of particularly interest, even though from time to time he's heard to let off a very loud, I believe you call it CURSING, noise when his golf ball goes for a little wander into the Enchanted Wood or comes to rest under the roots of the mighty oak. We are also very interested in his work in the crooked shed, particularly his inventions, and thought that they could prove useful. We have been looking to recruit him to the mission for some time."

"What is this mission," cried Phoebe," and how do you know my grandpa invents things?"

"Freddie Fox and his council members have been watching your grandpa for a long time. Freddie is a regular visitor to his garden and has even been in his shed watching him work on an invention called the Shrinkability Cupboard?" replied Slice with a curious smile. "I believe he has now successfully got it working, though it still requires a couple of modifications for it to achieve its true "labour-saving' capability."

Phoebe was both amazed and shocked as it was clear Slice knew an awful lot about recent events.

"Slice, why is this mission so important?" asked Phoebe.

"You don't have any brothers or sisters yet do you Phoebe, but in just another, 200 hundred or so, moon rises and sets, your mummy is going to give you a new baby sister," continued Slice.

"OOOHHH," squealed Phoebe, that would be so exciting but are you sure? How do you know? Although I have seen Mummy and Daddy looking in "Bumps R Us' a lot recently!"!"

"Oh yes, we are quite sure, Hare Henry has been speaking to a peaceful group of stars known as constellation Lyra. The brightest of all these stars is Erin and she is due to visit you soon. You will be her big sister and she will create a special place in your heart and a bond between sisters that can never be broken. Hare Henry is never wrong," said Slice emphatically.

"Wow that's fantastic news," squealed Phoebe, unable to contain her excitement.

"Just imagine when Erin arrives if she got lost on the way home from the hospital, and you were not able to play together or even see each other. You see Phoebe, I have a brother and sister and we were all born together and so like most golf balls, we are triplets. My brother and sister are Hook and Putty. Putty is the loveliest prettiest sister in the entire kingdom of the lost balls, and my brother Hook is just a born adventurer. The last time I heard from him he was on a golf course in Florida, having a fantastic underwater adventure with Jelly Fish Josh, and Jacob the Jolly Clown Fish."

"I don't understand," said Phoebe, "why don't you all live together as a family and why is your brother in such a happy place but your sister in such a terrible place?"

"Let me explain from the beginning. Why don't we go for a walk along the golf course, and I can show you a few things which will help me to explain our mission and I can also introduce you to some more of our friends," said Slice.

Phoebe listened intently, intrigued by what this mission could be, but she liked the way that Slice referred to "our friends"," almost as if Phoebe had a whole new gang of friends that she was just waiting to meet.

"Wait," said Phoebe, "I will just let Grandpa know where I am going and ask if I can take Swish for a walk, then you can explain everything." Grandpa had let Phoebe walk with Swish before, but he always watched her carefully through the crooked shed window, as it looked out over the golf course and the Enchanted Wood. Swish was an excellent bodyguard and took good care of Phoebe and would always drag her home if it was getting too late!

46

With Slice held tightly in her right hand, Swish's lead in the other, and of course her saxophone slung over her shoulder, Phoebe and Swish set off along the side of the golf course to the edge of the Enchanted Wood. After just a short while Phoebe and Swish sat down on the mossy bank by the side of the great oak tree and Slice began his story.

"On our way home from the golf ball birth factory myself, Hook and Putty were all neatly packaged in our brand new going home box, in the back of a transport lorry. Suddenly there was an almighty bang and our box crashed to the floor. Hook and I were fine but Putty rolled out of the box and out of the lorry bouncing down the motorway, laughing and waving to us as she went. At first, we thought this was good news because for golf balls there is nothing more exciting than to be free and bouncing into our next adventure. Golf balls love to play and explore, flying, bouncing, and then rolling along a lovely freshly cut strip of grass, surrounded by beautiful trees. We also get to meet and play with our wonderful animal friends that we live side by side with, in perfect peace and harmony. The golf course is our magnificent home. As golf balls, we are never exactly sure where we will come to a stop, or what will happen next. That is all part of the adventure waiting for the next exhilarating ping or whack when you are suddenly lifted into the air high above the trees to land in a completely new temporary holiday location."

"Do you have any control of where you go?" asked Phoebe who had been listening intently as Slice told his story?

"Yes, we have a mind of our own and we get energised once we are whacked by a golf club, or thingamajig as you call them. We can control our direction, by leaning one way or the other and keep moving by doing head over heels acrobatics as we bounce or roll along. We even get the wind to blow us and sometimes, our friends the animals will also join in the fun and pick us up and carry us to a more interesting place. I remember once when Percy Pigeon picked me up in his beak and lifted me so high, I was nearly touching the moon and then he let me go. I was flying so fast that when I hit the ground, I did my best bounce ever as Nel the Squirrel scooped me up and ran across the course into the edge of the Enchanted Wood and dropped me just under the roots of the great oak, just about where we are sitting now. Oh, how we laughed as we watched the golfers looking for me. It took ages for them to find me and only did when Bobby Badger ran out and practically threw me back, to play with them again," laughed Slice.

Phoebe and Swish were both laughing as they thought it was funny, in fact, it appeared that the whole of the Enchanted Wood and, even the gurgling stream, were joining in the laughter as they all listened to Slice.

"That sounds like a game of hide and seek that we play at Grandma's and Grandpas all the time said Phoebe. It sounds like you have a wonderful time playing and travelling around the golf course," added Phoebe.

Slice continued, "It's not just the golf course we get around, remember I told you about my brother Hook? Well, he is always looking for more exciting adventures, so he deliberately wanders off the course and joins the lost golf balls, who, though they call themselves that, are not really lost. They deliberately go where they will be found by a new person, who will then put them in their golf bag thinking that they are really clever and have found a new golf ball! They never realise the "lost golf balls' have planned it all along. Sometimes Bobby Badger and Freddie Fox listen to the golf people when they are talking about going on golfing holidays to far-off courses, or even countries, and so we often know where our friends are going on their next holiday. That's how I know that Hook is in Florida. I even had a friend who went to the Moon, with Neil Armstrong on Apollo11, but he has not got back yet, so Hare Henry is keeping a close eye on him."

Phoebe interrupted Slice as she had been wondering how he knew exactly where his brother Hook was. After all, it was not as if golf balls had mobile phones or could Bookface each other, could they?

"So how do you know Hook is in Florida?" asked Phoebe. "He could be anywhere by now."

"That's true," said Slice," but we send messages to each other regularly. It's quite easy really. Remember I said how here in the golf course all things work in harmony with nature? Well, if I want to get a message to Hook, I can ask the wind to carry it for me. He may pass it on to one of the regular bird couriers such as Percy Pigeon, who in turn will pass it onto Florida Flo the Flamingo, and she may ask Stingray Stella to deliver it to Hook depending on whether he's resting on a beach or swimming with Dougie Drake. It can take time, but the system works," explained Slice.

Bobcat Blake

Florida Flo

"That's amazing," said Phoebe. "So where is your sister then, what happened to her when she fell out of the delivery lorry?"

"That's just it," said Slice, "we thought she was off on an adventure, but she landed awkwardly on the very hard road and was likely injured or scuffed, as she bounced and rolled before she fell into a drain."

"Oh no that's terrible, we must go and help her,", said Phoebe.

"I'm afraid it is worse than that Phoebe. Putty lay in the drain injured for a while but was then eventually sucked up by a monster pipe sucker called a "road sweeper" and driven off to a recycling plant, where she was emptied into a great big tank full of mud and rubbish waiting to be cleaned. Over the next few weeks, we kept receiving messages from her, asking for help, and we were trying to organise a rescue plan but then disaster stuck. Putty was found and sent for recycling with plastic bottles, and if that was not bad enough the recycling plant is in Spain. She was separated from the plastic bottles and thrown into a bucket with lots of other poor balls, but only after she had a horrible red line painted on her. That was many moons ago and since then Putty has been condemned to a life in this terrible place. They call it the driving range!!!"

Chapter 7
The Mission

"We have to rescue Putty and bring her home, back to the Enchanted Wood, where she can play happily and be amongst all her friends and family," cried a very emotional Slice. Phoebe was sure she could see a small tear rolling down his number 2 nose.

"Don't cry Slice I will help and do whatever I can to get Putty home, but I am not sure how I can really. I mean how am I going to travel to Spain, find Putty and bring her home?" sighed Phoebe. "We need a plan. You say Freddie Fox is the wisest person, animal, or thing you know and that he had sanctioned this mission, so has he got a plan?" Phoebe asked.

Just then there was a rustling sound, from underneath the small bush just in front of Phoebe, as Bobby Badger appeared followed by Freddie Fox and several other animals that Phoebe did not recognise.

"Hello," said Freddie Fox, "welcome to the Enchanted Wood, our home. All these animals are members of The Animal Council and we have been working on a plan for some time. The great difficulty we have is that we need a human to play a key part in the plan and complete the mission."

"I see," said Phoebe, "well I am a human but surely it would be better if it was a grown-up, especially if we have to go to Spain to find Putty. Spain is a very big country. Do we know which driving range Putty is being held prisoner at, or how we are going to get her out? I don't speak very much Spanish either," added Phoebe who was suddenly feeling very nervous, "and I am only eight and two-thirds."

"Calm down Phoebe," said a very calm and thoughtful Bobby Badger. He peered out over the top of his glasses as if he was about to start reading a book. Phoebe thought how strange it was to see a Badger wearing glasses, but then again, this Badger was talking to her! Just then he produced a scroll made of what looked like an old golf umbrella with lots of doodles written on it and began to read out what appeared to be a plan.

"Firstly," began Bobby Badger, "the reason we have chosen you is that you have a kind heart, incredible determination to get things done, and are an excellent negotiator. Your Grandpa invents things that could be of great use to us, such as the Shrinkability Cupboard. Freddie Fox and I have been watching him for many moons and we know that he too has a kind and gentle heart and likes to help others, but there is just one problem and that is his age."

Phoebe seemed shocked, yes Grandpa was quite old, but he was not ancient, and he still had all his own hair and teeth and could play hide and seek with her for hours, and constantly running around after, and away from Grandma kept him very fit.

"You see Phoebe," interrupted Freddie Fox," once people become grown-ups they stop believing in things like magic and are not as open to new ideas, such as listening to animals and talking golf balls! I think your grandpa is slightly different: he is an inventor, so he has to believe in magic, even though he tries to explain everything through straightforward science or engineering."

"But he would be much better at going to Spain," shrieked Phoebe.

"Don't worry mon petit chou, we are all going to España," said an unmistakably French voice from above. Phoebe looked up to see Nel the Squirrel wearing her best French beret sat alongside Percy Pigeon looking down from a branch in the great oak. Phoebe did not speak much French, but she was comforted that Nel the Squirrel sounded very kind and reassuring, with a soft and gentle French accent. "I have volunteered for the mission as I used to be in the French Foreign Legion you know, and I also speak excellent Spanish. Como Estas?"

"Muy Bien," replied Phoebe understanding that Nel had just asked her how she was in Spanish, "but I think it would be much better if we all stuck to English golf ball animalese, or whatever it is we are speaking now, so we can all understand each other and the plan," added Phoebe.

"Well said, Phoebe. Please continue reading the plan Bobby," said Freddie Fox in his Headmaster and very much the Leader of the Council voice, as he called upon everyone present to listen very carefully to what Bobby Badger had to say next.

"The plan is very straightforward. Slice, Phoebe, Nel, and Freddie are all going to Spain, where they will find Putty and bring her home. Simples!" said Bobby.

Phoebe gasped, "That's not a plan, it's just what you want to do!"

There was complete silence, and everyone looked at Phoebe in admiration.

"Let's go back to the beginning. Firstly, we need to know where exactly in Spain Putty is. Can we send a message on the wind to find out?" Phoebe asked Freddie.

"Secondly, how are we all going to get to Spain and back? If we can work out how to do that, then we can think about the next part of the rescue, how we actually release Putty from the driving range."

"Phoebe is right," said Freddie. "Percy Pigeon go and fly on the wind now and send the message straightaway that we need the exact address where Putty is being held." With a sudden flap of his wings and an understanding coo, Percy was off to find the wind and pass on the important message. Freddie turned to Phoebe, staring straight into her eyes so that

Phoebe almost felt she was going under a spell as he spoke very slowly and precisely.

"We know that your grandpa and some of his friends are planning a golfing holiday to Spain, so we need to go with them, hidden inside their luggage, so we can sneak onto the Baggage Air flight to and from Spain. To do this we will need to get inside Grandpa's Shrinkability Cupboard, shrink down to golf ball size and hide in the Jolly Trolley golf bag."

"Swish, it will be your job to get us all out of the cupboard and into the golf bag once we are shrunk. Do you think you can manage that?" asked Freddie. "Woof, woof, I can," said Swish wagging his tail obediently.

"Swish you can talk, why did you not tell me before?" asked Phoebe stroking a very happy Swish.

"Phoebe you will control the de-shrinking process with your saxophone once we are all safely back here with Putty,", continued Freddie Fox.

"Does this mean I am going to be shrunk too and go with you to España?" exclaimed Phoebe.

"I'm afraid so," said Freddie. "This mission needs bravery and courage if it is to succeed and that is why I am coming with you, Nel and Slice. Bobby will stay here and take care of all the council business in my absence and take over as leader, should I not return! Just one last thing Phoebe, we will need to be able to return to normal size once we are in Spain, so we can work on the rescue, but then be able to shrink back so we can travel home. This means that you must make sure that the shrinkability process works and that all of your Grandpa's modifications are correct and tested, after all, we do want to get back to our normal size, don't we," said Freddie cautiously.

"Oh, we certainly do," said Phoebe trying to be brave, but she was quite worried about being shrunk down to the size of a golf ball, packed into a golf bag, smuggled onboard Baggage Air, flying to Spain, returning to normal size, rescuing Putty, shrinking back down to miniature size and getting smuggled back home. What could possibly go wrong!!!

Chapter 8
Grandpa's Minor Modifications

Grandpa was sitting in his favourite lounge chair reading the Lymm Bugle when Phoebe crashed into the room. She could not stop thinking, or should we say worrying, about the mission to rescue Putty and the daring plan that sounded like it still needed a lot of work. She knew that somehow, she had to get Grandpa to make some important modifications to the Shrinkability Cupboard that would enable her to return to normal size, but then to shrink herself again without going into the cupboard. There must be a way to achieve this, after all, Grandpa had said it "was just simple molecular physics" but simple or not Phoebe had to have a way of shrinking back down after the rescue, so she could get back into the golf bag with Slice, and hopefully Putty, Nel, and Freddie.

"Grandpa, do you think you could explain molecular physics to me?" Phoebe asked Grandpa deciding that the best way to bring up the subject was head-on.

"Well, it's a simple derivative of the combination of Bernoulli's principle, Newton's Third Law, and The Theory of Relativity, why do you ask?" said Grandpa to a very confused Phoebe!

"Well, I was just thinking how much more labour could be saved by the Shrinkability Cupboard if you could shrink something, say for example your Jolly Trolley, then you could just put it in your pocket or in your suitcase when you fly off on holiday, say perhaps to Spain, make them normal size whilst you are on holiday (in Spain) and then shrink them back again to bring them home, from Spain," said Phoebe, convinced that if she kept repeating Spain as a holiday destination it would make Grandpa want to book it.

"Hmm," pondered Grandpa, "I can see how that could have great advantages to the travel industry for moving all kinds of things around the world. That is a very good idea Pheebs. I will apply some of the old grey matter to the problem and see what I can come up with." Phoebe was not sure what he meant by old grey matter but guessed it was brain power!

With that Grandpa set off jauntily towards his shed with Swish following close behind, never wanting to miss something interesting. The next few hours led to much crashing and banging, with more than the occasional bout of cursing coming out of the crooked shed. Suddenly the door swung open, and Swish ran out as fast as his legs would carry him. "Swish come here I need a volunteer," shouted Grandpa, hot on his heels.

Grandpa came into the kitchen carrying a new control panel for the Shrinkability Cupboard. With his glasses in the correct place, his long fingers set to work to replace the old button with a control panel that had three settings, SHRINK, EXTENDED REVERSIBLE SHRINK, and MERGE.

"I think this will do everything we want it to do now Pheebs," said a very pleased-looking Grandpa. "I have added another control that creates a merge function."

"But what will that do, and how does the EXTENDED REVERSIBLE SHRINK, work?" asked a very interested but puzzled Phoebe, as she knew that the ability to reverse the shrink without using the Shrinkability Cupboard was going to be vital if they were going to get to Spain and back undetected, as well as the minor issue of rescuing Putty.

"Pheebs, I have given your ideas about the world transport industry some considerable thought. You were right, the ability to resize back to normal but then to be able to reshrink later is important. When families go on holiday, they can shrink all their suitcases down to the size of,", Grandpa looked around for something small to make the comparison when he noticed one of his golf balls sat on Fiver, the kitchen table, "a golf ball," he cried, "and then they just put it in their pocket and off they go to wherever and resize using the same molecular reconstruction. Sorry Pheebs, that's Three Blind Mice. At the end of the holiday, they simply play the same molecular deconstruction tune, Three Blind Mice, in reverse to reshrink it back for the journey home. This means that anyone will be able to travel with a suitcase full of clothes in their pocket. This will mean that planes can be smaller and use much less fuel, so becoming more eco-friendly and helping to save the planet," explained Grandpa enthusiastically.

"I don't think Baggage Air will like it as they won't be able to charge you for luggage," laughed Grandpa, obviously very pleased with himself.

"Grandpa that's brilliant, and I actually understand all of that, but what about the merge?" asked Phoebe.

"Well, I suddenly thought," replied Grandpa, "what about things that always go together like rhubarb and custard, or roast beef and Yorkshire pudding, you could just merge them together and save even more time?" That seemed a very good idea to me. "That reminds me I'm hungry and I need something to eat before I play golf, how do you fancy some fish, chips, and curry from the Chinese takeaway? I don't know where Grandma has got to."

Hand in hand Phoebe and Grandpa skipped out of the back door and headed off to the chippy, leaving behind a sleeping Swish in his basket under Five the table. They didn't see Grandma just leaving Mrs Bridges back door and squeezing through the large gap in the garden fence. Grandma came into the kitchen just as the naughty Fiver was annoying Swish by extending his fifth leg and kicking Swish's basket. The kick was so hard it caused the other legs to jump up in the air and the golf ball that Grandpa had left on Fiver rolled off, bouncing on the floor and up onto the door of the Shrinkability Cupboard. The door flew open just as the golf ball bounced again and Grandma dived forward trying to catch it with her left hand but as she tried to regain her balance, she accidentally grabbed the control panel with her right hand, turning the dial to MERGE as she stumbled into the cupboard and the door closed shut behind her!

The Shrinkability Cupboard began to whirr and vibrate and shake quite violently with Grandma inside still holding tight to the golf ball. Actually, Grandma was feeling quite proud of herself, thinking that the last time she had made a catch like that was when she was in the Under 11s rounders team. Strangely Grandma thought she had joined one of those roller coaster rides at the fairground, as her tummy felt very peculiar, and she was sure she was shrinking. Everything suddenly went very black and quiet. After a couple of minutes, she noticed that the cupboard door was slightly ajar, and she was able to roll towards it. Before she realised, Grandma was rolling and then bouncing out of the cupboard and onto the kitchen floor, to be greeted by a very large dog sniffing and licking her. But Grandma could not feel anything, because she was inside the golf ball and the large dog was that "good for nothing mutt, Swish!"

Swish and Fiver had seen what had happened and realised that they had caused this terrible accident. Grandma had not only been shrunk to the size of a golf ball, but she was actually merged into it! She might have been trapped but Swish and Fiver could hear her making promises of what she was going to do to both them and Grandpa when she got out of this "stupid invention of Goooooooooorddddoooooooooooooooons!" Yep, she was very cross!

Just then Grandpa and Phoebe arrived back home having eaten their lunch in the chippy, as Grandpa was in a rush as he was late for a "sneaky round of golf with my mates".

Grandpa spotted a golf ball on the kitchen floor, lying next to a very still, but guilty-looking Fiver. He quickly picked it up before throwing it into his golf bag and dashing off to play. "See you later, Pheebs, must run, Grandma should be back soon," and with that, he was gone.

Swish was desperately trying to hide from Phoebe, who was currently searching the house and shouting for him and Grandma. He was terrified as he knew that Grandma was about to play golf with Grandpa, not as his partner, but as his golf ball!!!

He had to come clean and tell Phoebe what had happened. Now they had to rescue Grandma too.

Chapter 9
Grandma's Round of Golf

Swish was barking uncontrollably and chasing his tail as fast as he could, desperately trying to work out what he could do. How could he tell Phoebe what had happened to Grandma, who at this very moment, was on her way to the golf course inside one of Grandpa's golf balls??

Phoebe returned from looking for Grandma at Bridges Mrs next door, but even after wiping away the soggy "Wee kisses" and straightening her hat, she still couldn't see any sign of Grandma. "What on earth is the matter Swish, calm down. Bark slowly so I can understand you!" said Phoebe.

"Woof, woof not my fault, grr, it was that stupid table Fiver that did it grr," said Swish, has now slowed down to just a blur." He was kicking my basket and made the golf ball fall off and Grandma dove to catch it, which she did brilliantly, but then fell into the cupboard and shrunk."

"Oh no," said Phoebe, "Quick all I need to do is play Three Blind Mice to her, where is she Swish?"

"Woof, in the golf ball, that's now in Grandpa's bag, who is now at the golf course for a 'sneaky round of golf with his mates'!!!"

"What! screamed Phoebe. Are you telling me that Grandpa's new Merge function has put Grandma in the golf ball! and Grandpa has gone to play golf with her, and he doesn't know!"!"

"Yes, that's what I'm barking at," said Swish.

"Now is not the time to decide whose fault this dreadful calamity is! We need to save Grandma quickly! How can we get a message to The Animal Council in the Enchanted Wood to get them to help us?" cried Phoebe.

Swish and Fiver looked very sorry for themselves as Phoebe scowled at them. Just then Fiver stretched his leg, making it grow to several metres, straight out of the back door and into the apple tree. Charlie Chaffinch hopped onto the new branch and started whistling with Fiver. When Phoebe and Swish listened a little harder, they could hear that Fiver was giving very specific instructions for Charlie to take to The Animal Council. This was no ordinary trunk call, it was a full-blown emergency and within seconds Charlie was on his way, already passing the message to the wind who had overheard some of it and was now blowing Charlie, at lightspeed, to the Enchanted Wood where a meeting with Freddie Fox and all the council had already been called.

"Hello, Mr T Starter," said Grandpa, "It all seems very quiet today. Where are all your animal friends, have they gone on holiday?"

"You're right Mr Shortshanks, it is quiet. There was a huge kerfuffle a couple of minutes ago and everyone disappeared, very strange indeed. Mark my words something is going on. Anyway, enjoy your game. Off you go when you're ready," said Mr T Starter, wiggling his huge handlebar moustache.

Grandpa reached his long fingers into the golf bag on the Jolly Trolley, pulled the first golf ball out, and placed it on top of the tee peg, ready to play his shot. Grandma was horrified as she looked out from the golf ball and stared down the length of the first fairway. Suddenly there was a great whack on her bottom and Grandma was flying up into the sky, spinning as she went and feeling the rush of the wind as it flew past her ears, whilst holding tight to the inner walls of the ball.

The views were spectacular. Grandma was in a trance as she had never realised how beautiful the golf course and the village where she lived was. Grandma had never felt more alive and though a little nervous she certainly wasn't scared. Suddenly she started to descend, rather like a plane coming into land, except it was not a smooth landing at all. In fact, poor old Grandma bounced several times before she started spinning and rolling down the fairway. Head over heels she went, making her quite dizzy and setting her tummy into a spin. Then it all stopped, and everything was still. Grandma was lying on her back staring up at the sky, wondering if she was dreaming.

Meanwhile back at the great oak, Freddie Fox was organising the rescue. "Pay attention everyone," said Freddie in his best Leader of the Council voice, "We must divert Grandma to the great oak tree roots where Nel the Squirrel can gather her up and bring her back here to the mossy bank. We can look after her until Phoebe and her saxophone can get here. I need eyes in the sky. Percy Pigeon can you coordinate with the wind to drive her to the roots, please? I estimate that Grandpa Shortshanks will make at least five more shots before we have a chance to implement any diversions to the great oak, which means that there is a chance of Grandma landing in the pond by the fourth green. Charlie Chaffinch go and tell Dougie Drake and his underwater teams to be on standby for an unexpected visitor," said Freddie Fox as he issued orders quickly and calmly, but inwardly he was rather worried especially if Grandma came down in the pond which was a bit smelly!

Grandma was just about getting her bearings when she heard the familiar voice of Grandpa approaching with his friends, who all seemed to be making complimentary noises about "what a jolly good shot that was". Before Grandma could shout, "Goooooordon," there was a great whoosh and Grandma was up flying once more. She was starting to think that despite the original shock this was quite good fun, and she was beginning to enjoy it. In the distance, Grandma could see her house and the crooked shed, which was rather exciting as she had never seen them before from so high in the sky. Just then she noticed that "good for nothing mutt", Swish the Dog pulling Phoebe, and her saxophone as if his life depended on it. Little did she realise that it was her life that depended on it!

Grandma was just preparing herself for another landing bounce and a roll when she suddenly she came to a very gentle stop, finding herself up to her golf ball waist in sand." Oh, that reminds me, I need a holiday if I ever get out of this mess," she said muttering to herself. Then she remembered that today was Wednesday and that meant it was the Women's Institute meeting and Coronation Street on telly. She needed to get out of this predicament quickly, after all, she was a respectable Grandma, not a golf ball!

Phoebe, Swish, and Slice, who were now living deep inside Phoebe's pocket, had now arrived at the mossy embankment by the great oak, where Freddie Fox was waiting. He quickly updated them. "The latest report from the eye in the sky, Percy Pigeon, has confirmed that Grandma had just landed in, or was it on, the nearby beach. Everyone is on standby to make the rescue on the next shot."

Grandpa approached the sandy bunker with his wedge thingamajig, as Phoebe called it. "Right just a gentle toss up into the air should do the trick," said Grandpa to no one in particular but loud enough to drown out Grandma's screams of "Gooooooooooooorrrrrrrrrrdon" as she flew out of the sand heading for a nice soft landing on the lovely smooth green carpet of grass.

"Noo, Noo Now!" cooed Percy Pigeon to the wind, just as Grandma emerged from the sand, "Blow, blow." Suddenly there was a huge gust and it appeared to Grandma that she was on an invisible magic carpet and being gently carried towards a large tree, in the completely opposite direction. With a gentle bump, she landed by the roots of the great oak, and before she could blink a squirrel had picked her up in her cheeks and was running with her to the edge of the wood, where she could see Swish and Phoebe waiting.

"Blood and stomach pills," cried Grandpa," where has that ball gone now? I swear they have a mind of their own!"

Phoebe quickly played Three Blind Mice to reverse the shrinking process, and a very relieved but confused Grandma reappeared holding a golf ball. Somewhat muddy, and not sure why she was on the golf course walking with Swish and Phoebe, she maintained that she had wanted to ask Grandpa what he wanted for his dinner!!!

"Well done team, excellent rescue work," said Freddie Fox to a very pleased-looking bunch of animals, trees, and wind. "A good example of nature working together."

Chapter 10
A Golfing Holiday

In just a few days Grandma seemed to be over her ordeal as a golf ball, but her recent contact with the sandy beach had strengthened her resolve to persuade Grandpa to take a holiday. There was no better time than the next couple of weeks, as it was half-term holidays and Grandpa's birthday. "What better present than to play a round of golf with your Granddaughter, whilst I lay by the side of a pool having a nice drinkie drink and a piece of cake," Grandma muttered to herself.

"Gordon, darling," began Grandma, "I think we should have a holiday to celebrate your birthday." Grandpa immediately knew that Grandma was after something as that was the first time since he had bought her a new cardigan last year, she had called him just the standard Gordon with no screeching extension to it. And as for the 'darling' bit, he honestly couldn't remember the last time.

"Well," said Grandpa, "I was talking to Mr T Starter earlier today and he was telling me that some chaps from the golf club had just returned from a fabulous place in Spain. It's called La Manga, and they were so impressed they have given it a five-star rating on Fabtrips.com."

What Grandpa and Grandma did not know was that Freddie Fox and Bobby Badger had received word back from La Manga Lola, the leader of the parakeets, in a message brought by the wind to Percy Pigeon, that Putty had been found but she remained trapped inside the golf ball prison, the La Manga driving range!

Nel the Squirrel had used her magic French accent to cast a spell over Mr T Starter, to make sure that he passed on her comments about how good La Manga was to Grandpa, knowing that Grandpa always took Mr T at his word.

"That settles it," said Grandma "we're going down to Current Buns, the travel agents today and booking a nice villa and flights on Baggage Air. And, I want a reserved seat," added Grandma.

Grandpa knew there was little point in arguing and besides, he had to agree that playing golf in La Manga with Phoebe would be the perfect birthday present. Later that afternoon they both went down to Current Buns to book, "the trip of a lifetime" as Grandma had now taken to calling it, just in case Grandpa started to get second thoughts!

Phoebe was looking forward to this weekend's visit to Grandma and Grandpa's as Mummy Shortshanks Brodrick had said, "You can stay for the weekend, on the condition they don't convert you into a member of a strange cult." Mummy really did not like her grandparents, which Phoebe could never understand, as they were the kindest people in the whole wide world.

Just as soon as she arrived at the 'crooked shed' Charlie Chaffinch whistled a message, "you are needed at an urgent meeting of The Animal Council. Come straight away!"

71

Phoebe quickly dropped her weekend bag, hugged Grandma, and grabbed Swish.

"I am just going to take Swish for a quick walk. I will only be a couple of minutes," she said and was off out of the back door just as Grandma was saying "We have a taxi booked to the airport in half an hour, we are going on a surprise birthday treat for Grandpa!" she shouted, unsure if Swish or Phoebe, who were already halfway to the Enchanted Wood, had heard her.

FREDDIE FOX

Freddie Fox and all The Animal Council were waiting eagerly for Phoebe and Swish to arrive at the mossy embankment by the side of the Enchanted Wood. Phoebe and Swish were both out of breath as they took their seats and Freddie began to speak. Phoebe took Slice out of her pocket, where he had been living safely for the last week, so he could hear the latest news of his sister Putty clearly.

"As most of you will know we have been working very closely with our friends across Europe. Despite the recent human difficulties that seem to be happening, we have had great success in locating Putty in La Manga, Spain. We have established a very good relationship with La Manga Lola, who is the leader of the parakeets, and she is very keen to help us. Grandpa and Grandma Shortshanks have been persuaded (by Nel the Squirrel and her magic spell over Mr T Starter) that this weekend would be an excellent time to take a short holiday to La Manga. The bad news is the taxi is booked in just 27 minutes, so we have very little time. The good news is that Phoebe has been invited on the trip, so she will not have to be shrunk and travel with Nel and I hidden in the Jolly Trolley," said Freddie Fox with great authority. Phoebe, you, Nel, Swish, and I must get back to Grandma and Grandpa's house quickly. Swish you must create a diversion and get Grandpa and Grandma out of the kitchen so Nel and I can get into the Shrinkability Cupboard and then hide away in Jolly Trolley. Any questions?" asked Freddie Fox.

"Woof, woof let's go," said Swish impatiently.

Slice could not help smiling at all his friends helping him to rescue his sister. "Thank you, thank you, thank you" was all he could say and think.

Grandma was rushing around trying to squeeze a last piece of cake into her handbag, and Grandpa was carrying the suitcases to the front door as Swish ran in barking uncontrollably at Grandma and tugging at her skirt like as a dog possessed. Grandma tried to whack Swish with the kitchen brush and was chasing him out of the kitchen into the hallway. "Wait until I get hold of you, you stupid mutt," shrieked Grandma. Just as the brush was about to hit Swish's tail, he leapt up at Grandpa who fell backwards over the suitcase, tripping Grandma up in the process. It was chaos but a brilliant diversion!

"Quick," said Phoebe opening the Shrinkability Cupboard as Freddie Fox and Nel the Squirrel jumped in. "One last thing Phoebe," said Freddie Fox, make sure you get the controls correct! I really do not want to be merged with Nel today as no one wants to be a Foxy Squirrel!"

With that, Phoebe slammed the door, turned the dial to EXTENDED REVERSIBLE SHRINK. Within a couple of seconds, Phoebe had both Nel and Freddie in the palm of her hand and placed them carefully in the Jolly Trolley who was standing to attention by the kitchen door.

Phoebe rushed into the hall just in time to save Swish from Grandma and to help Grandpa back to his feet." I will just drop him off at Mrs Bridges for the weekend," said Phoebe.

"Ask her to turn him into sausages," shouted Grandma, adjusting her cardigan and skirt. "Grandma!" shouted Phoebe, as she carried Swish out of harm's way. "Well done Swish that was a brilliant diversion but quickly the taxi is here."

By the time Phoebe was back, after getting the usual sloppy WEE kiss on the cheek from Mrs Bridges, Grandma was already in the front seat of the taxi and Grandpa had loaded the baggage and Jolly Trolley into the boot. Grandma had been most insistent that Grandpa was not allowed to shrink the Jolly Trolley, and carry it in his pocket, as she did not want anything to go wrong (following her recent experience as a golf ball!). "Let the adventure begin," said Grandpa excitedly. How right you are thought, Phoebe!

The airport was very busy but relatively uneventful, apart from when they put the bags and the Jolly Trolley onto the conveyor belt and a golf ball fell out. Phoebe rushed forward "Let me just check all the pockets are zipped shut Grandpa we don't want anything else falling out, do we?" she said nervously checking all the pockets but especially the one where Nel and Freddie were travelling, most definitely in baggage class. A small voice with a French accent was heard in a whisper, "très bien, ma chérie", as the Jolly Trolley disappeared down the conveyor belt and onto the plane. Once inside the luggage hold of the plane Nel the Squirrel was keen to explore and desperate to perform some acrobatic jumps, from bag to bag, but Freddie Fox was adamant that for the next couple of hours they were staying put. "We need to stay here and rest," he said. "We have work to do when we land. This is not a holiday for us Nel, we have to rescue Putty and we are not taking any risks."

" Oh really, here we are shrunk to the size of a golf ball, packed inside a Jolly Trolley and smuggled on board a flight to Spain! No risk, eh, oh là là!" replied Nel the Squirrel as she reluctantly sat back down in her corner of the pocket.

Meanwhile above in the cabin, Phoebe and her grandparents were sitting comfortably. The flight was just long enough for Grandma to eat all her cake, and for Grandpa to have a "short kip" with a very loud snore! In no time at all the captain in a muffled voice, advised passengers to "please return to your seats as we are landing in the tropical paradise of La Manga".

As the plane landed it bounced, ever so slightly, but enough for Grandma's tummy to get a funny feeling she was a golf ball again but as the plane came to halt, Grandma decided it was probably that she had eaten too much cake!

Phoebe stepped off the plane to be met by a sudden rise in temperature, even hot enough for Grandma to remove her cardigan on the aeroplane steps. The glorious sunshine, blue skies and gently waving palm trees were beautiful. Grandpa and Grandma looked very happy and excited for their "trip of a lifetime".".

Grandma stood in the queue waiting for the luggage whilst recounting stories of how many bags they had lost on their various holidays over the years. It made Phoebe very nervous, as they waited for the bags and above all the Jolly Trolley with Freddie Fox and Nel the Squirrel hidden inside.

One by one all the bags arrived and were claimed by the owners, but even after the last bag had been reclaimed there was no sign of the Jolly Trolley. "Where can THEY be?" asked a very tearful Phoebe as the now empty carousel came to a stop. "I mean him, the Jolly Trolley," Phoebe blubbered, trying to cover up her concerns.

"There it is," shouted Grandpa pointing to the Jolly Trolley who was standing to attention, waiting patiently by the door for them to join him. Phoebe ran over and whispered, "everyone OK in there?"

"Muy Bien y tu?" was the excited reply as Nel the Squirrel practiced her best Spanish (which translated means 'very well and you?'), and with that everyone and everything jumped into the taxi for the short ride to the villa where they were staying.

Chapter 11
Reconnaissance

Phoebe held Slice gently in her pocket, ensuring he was always near as if to reinforce that this was not a holiday but the most important mission that either of them would ever undertake in their lives.

It was only a short journey from the airport, but Phoebe could not get over how deep blue and friendly the sky looked. It was almost as if it was welcoming her and offering any help it could. As she stared up into the sky, she noticed that a flock of birds seemed to be following them. These were no ordinary birds and with the greatest respect to Percy Pigeon and Charlie Chaffinch. Whilst they were both extraordinary birds, you could not describe them as beautiful. These birds, a mixture of blue, green, and yellow feathers with large red beaks were truly beautiful as they swooped and soared escorting the taxi to the villa. At the head of the flock was the most beautiful of all the birds, La Manga Lola, the leader of the parakeets.

Within minutes of arriving at the large white villa that was to be home for the next few days, Grandma had chosen the bedrooms and made herself extremely comfortable on one of the many large sunbeds by the side of the pool. Meanwhile, Grandpa had unloaded the taxi, with the help of Phoebe, and had put the Jolly Trolley in a room called the "buggy store" and placed all the luggage in the correct bedrooms. It was a little strange as all the bedrooms were downstairs and the kitchen and lounge were upstairs! It seemed that the villa was an upside-down house, downstairs was upstairs, and upstairs was downstairs.

"Time for a beer said Grandpa," as he ventured out onto the upstairs terrace. "Oh, look Pheebs we have our own little bar, just perfect," said Grandpa as he opened a nice cold can of beer and shouted down to where he could see Grandma by the pool, "time for a drinkie drink", raising the can above his head as he did so.

Phoebe went to explore downstairs and change into her swimming costume, so she could swim in the cool turquoise water of the pool.

Meanwhile back in the buggy store, some heavy murmurings were coming from Jolly Trolley as Freddie Fox and Nel the Squirrel was still stuck deep inside the pocket. "Surely Phoebe can't have forgotten us," complained Freddie Fox, "we need to be spending time on reconnaissance to work out how we are going to rescue Putty, and we must meet with La Manga Lola as soon as possible. We have no time to waste. What is Phoebe doing?"

Phoebe was enjoying her swim when the most beautiful parakeet flew down and landed by the side of the pool. "Hola, you must be Phoebe, I'm La Manga Lola. Where are Freddie Fox and Nel the Squirrel, I understood they were travelling with you?"

"Oh no!" cried Phoebe, "I almost forgot them," and with that Phoebe was out of the pool and running into her downstairs bedroom to dry off and grab her saxophone so she could perform the molecular reconstruction and bring them back to normal size.

"I'm so sorry," said Phoebe as she carefully pulled Freddie and Nel from the pocket of Jolly Trolley and carried them downstairs. Placing them on the bed next to Slice, she quickly played Three Blind Mice and watched in amazement as with a shake and a shudder of their bushy tails, Freddie and Nel returned to their normal size.

"Merci or should I say gracias?" said a very grateful Nel who immediately ran up the curtains, had a stretch and a good look around the bedroom, before jumping onto the rotating fan in the centre of the ceiling and landing back down on the bed a little quicker than she had expected.

"Settle down Nel," said Freddie Fox, "we have no time to waste. We need to find La Manga Lola and work out where we are going to stay whilst we are here, now we are back to our normal size" Freddie said with a hard stare at Phoebe who did look a little guilty about her momentary memory lapse.

Phoebe opened the bedroom door that led onto the terrace where La Manga Lola was sitting. "This is Lola the leader of the parakeets," said Phoebe, hoping to get back in Freddie Fox's good books as he and Nel quickly ran from the bedroom and scurried out of sight under the sunbeds, as "the need for secrecy is paramount to the success of this mission," said Freddie reinforcing his authority.

Lola explained that there was a large barranca, that ran at the back of the villa and led directly onto the golf course. It meant they could easily travel back and forth safely and out of sight. Phoebe looked a little confused, "What on earth is a barranca?" she asked.

"A dry riverbed," answered Nel, in a perfect Spanish accent, rather than her normal French one.

"Follow me,", said Lola, "Phoebe you need to stay here so as not to raise any suspicion. We'll come back later with news of Putty." Lola led the way flying low and slowly to enable Freddie and Nel to keep up. Slice had to stay behind as well, as it would be too risky for him to be on the golf course, after all, they were here to rescue his sister, not for him to get lost.

"What should I be doing?" asked Phoebe who was far from happy at not being involved in this part of the mission, as surely this was going to be the exciting bit.

"Have a good look around here and see if you can make friends with some of the locals and anyone you think might prove useful to us. Make sure that you have wrapped your birthday present for Grandpa," said Freddie Fox trying to placate Phoebe whilst running to keep up with Lola and Nel.

After a few minutes, the intrepid trio arrived at the golf course, which was every bit as beautiful as their home course back at the Enchanted Wood but lined by hundreds of palm trees that Nel the Squirrel thought were very boring as they had no branches, just a straight trunk, and a hairy head and were not very good for climbing and acrobatics. Freddie Fox could not understand where Nel got her energy from, as she repeatedly ran up to the top of each tree where it was possible to see the entire golf course stretching out in front of them. Lola flew ahead and guided them towards the place where Putty was being held.

Suddenly the entire mood of the course changed from a lovely, open, sunny place to a dark, miserable area completely enclosed by high netted walls and a roof. In each corner, there were high floodlights that were permanently switched on to give light but were also searching for anyone or anything trying to escape. This was a place where the sun never shone and even the sky had large black angry clouds that threatened to deposit huge torrents of rain onto the miserable inhabitants below. Every day was the same for the poor unfortunate golf balls trapped inside.

Freddie and Nel crawled out from the safety of the barranca and cautiously approached the prison fence. Suddenly Freddie was shocked as Lola dive-bombed down at great speed and landed on his head "Stop, don't touch the netting!" she shouted, "It's an electric fence. The charge is so strong that even the great wild boars, that live in the forest cannot burrow through," Lola pointed out the remote-controlled, sad-looking, driverless, tractor that spent its entire day driving up and down, scooping balls up into its basket and taking them back to the dark house in the corner. There the golf balls were emptied into a big bucket and tipped back into another noisy clanging machine, before being squeezed out one at a time only to be whacked back to where they had just come from. The short flight through the cage was the only relief the poor balls got from the boredom that sent some of them quite mad.

"How do we get in there Lola?" asked Freddie Fox feeling overwhelmed by the task facing them. "That's just it," said Lola, "there is no way in and no way out. It is a completely enclosed prison cell with no animals, apart from the occasional small worm, living there. The wild boars, who are extremely strong but just as stupid, thought that the balls were chocolates and decided to mount a raid one evening trying to burrow underneath the nets. Since then, the fences have been electrified and so even members of the parakeets can't sit anywhere on the fencing without being turned into a very well-done parakeet burger!"

"There has to be a way in," said Freddie thoughtfully," any thoughts Nel?"

"Well, when I was in the French Foreign Legion, we often came across minefields that also had electrified fences around them. The only way we could get through was by sending a tank in first and then the troops and I would follow behind, which is not very helpful really is it?"

"No not really," said Freddie, wishing that Nel would stop going on about her days in the French Foreign Legion. He was starting to wonder why he had brought her. Perhaps she was not as clever as he thought!

Back at the villa Phoebe had made friends with a small blond-haired boy called Jonty, who was staying next door and had accidentally kicked his football over the hedge and into the pool. It made a great splash all over Grandma who woke up with a scream from her "little afternoon nap".

"Oh, I'm awfully sorry," said Jonty "I was just practising my penalty shots and it went straight through the gap in the hedge. It must have been a good shot though, I'm not sure Messi could have done that," he said cheekily. "I am on holiday, and I have football lessons every morning and golf lessons every afternoon, so I have to practice whenever and wherever I can."

"The golf lessons sound really exciting,", said Phoebe, "can anyone go?"

Jonty explained that his next golf lesson was in an hour and Phoebe could come and watch if she liked, but she had to promise to be quiet, so he could concentrate on whacking the balls back at the driving range. Jonty thought all girls talked far too much.

"Did you say driving range," screamed Phoebe realising that Jonty was one of those "locals" that Freddie Fox had told her to find and make friends with. Jonty clearly knew his way around and would know how to get to where Putty was being held! She could not wait to tell Freddie and Nel the exciting news. Surely this rescue was going to be easier than anyone thought, as all she had to do was look through the balls whilst Jonty had his lesson and find Putty with her distinctive number 3 nose and rosy complexion. How difficult could it be!

As Phoebe was waiting for Jonty to go and get his golf clubs there was a rustling noise coming from the barranca at the back of the pool. Lola swooped down, almost knocking Phoebe's hat off, and then she saw Nel and Freddie hiding just

under the sunbeds. They did not look very happy and so Phoebe knew that the reconnaissance mission had not gone well even before Freddie gave her a full update and Nel set out the problems of the electric fence and netting.

Phoebe told everyone about Jonty and that she was going with him to the driving range. "Surely this

must be good news," she said to no one in particular, trying to
lift the mood.

Chapter 12
The Rescue

Jonty and Phoebe skipped off to the golf lesson, Jonty carrying a small bag of golf clubs swung over his shoulder. To get to the golf course they only had to walk across the barranca and over the fairway, where they were greeted by José, the golf teacher. He led them through the golf shop and past a sliding door that opened automatically as they approached and closed behind them with a swoosh. Once the door had closed the hustle and bustle of the shop and all the brightly coloured golf accessories on display, disappeared and everything was very quiet and still. They were in a small concrete room with several small bays with just a green mat on the floor, and what looked like a garage door. A small rusty pipe protruded from the wall with a metal cage-like basket underneath it. José produced a card from his pocket and held it near the rusty pipe. Suddenly the garage door started to roll itself up into the ceiling and the pipe began spitting golf balls into the basket. Phoebe realised they were looking out onto the driving range. It was deathly quiet with no movement or sound at all. It was rather like visiting a graveyard after dark. Phoebe was uncomfortable in this unfriendly place and turned to see if she could run back into the shop. The door was well and truly closed with no obvious way out and not even a window. It was indeed a golf ball prison.

Just beyond the garage doors was a set of gates that led to the back of the barranca. Phoebe noticed a big red button with a sign saying,

IN EMERGENCY PUSH TO OPEN

"That might come in very handy," she muttered to herself.

Jonty was going through a series of what he called "practice swings" with José, and whilst it looked quite impressive, he was not hitting any balls and Phoebe really couldn't see the point of it at all. The silence was really starting to drive Phoebe quite bonkers until she could stand it no more and said, "José, can I have some balls?"?

"Of course, help yourself to those in the basket in the corner."

This was the perfect opportunity for Phoebe to start searching for Putty, but as she searched through the basket there was no sign." Here Jonty hit these balls and I will get you some more from the basket." Phoebe was delivering balls as quickly as she could to Jonty who was now expertly whacking them out onto the driving range just as quickly as Phoebe could supply them, but there was still no sign of Putty. Jonty was very hot and needed a rest, but Phoebe was determined to empty the bucket in her quest to find Putty. Just when she thought they were making some progress, José waved a magic card near the rusty pipe and more golf balls appeared, which he then emptied into the bucket. This was hopeless, thought Phoebe, there are thousands of balls, and we will never get through them all, besides there are several thousand more just lying out on the range waiting to be picked up by the sad-looking, tractor.

Meanwhile at the far end of the driving range, behind the netting, Freddie Fox and Nel the Squirrel were watching intently from the top of the barranca trying to work out a way in, as they clearly couldn't just march through the shop during the day, and it was closed at night. Deep in thought, they watched as Jonty and Phoebe finished their lesson and set off home across the golf course.

"This is hopeless," said Freddie Fox, "even with Phoebe and her friend Jonty inside the cage, there are just too many golf balls for them ever to find Putty. We would need an army to check every ball and we just don't have the time." Just then Nel the Squirrel piped up "Eureka, that's it!" Freddie looked at her, remembering that a Eureka moment was when a famous Greek scientist (Archimedes) realised that the water displacement volume when he sat in a bath naked, was the same as his volume. Freddie failed to see how an image of a naked Greek man running around shouting Eureka, Greek for 'I have found it', was going to help!

"Oh no, here we go again on some other useless French Foreign Legion story," he grumbled.

"This situation is very similar to the battle for Paris, that I was personally involved in when I was in the Legion you know."

Freddie was about to scream when Lola said, "We should all hear what Nel has to say before we dismiss it." Freddie nodded in agreement, as at that moment things were looking very black, as was the sky. A huge storm was gathering over the driving range. "If you have a plan Nel let's hear it," said Freddie Fox in a disgruntled and frustrated voice.

Nel the Squirrel began in her very French accent, after making sure that her battle beret was positioned perfectly. "If we are to find and liberate any, or all, of the golf balls we need to attack, leading with our heavy artillery, the tanks, and then once the barricades have been torn down, we will send in the army to search and liberate!"!"

Freddie Fox interrupted as he grew increasingly frustrated with Nel and her plan. "Will you speak in simple English, so we can all understand," he growled.

"I am speaking English, it is just my French accent," said Nel," but I will try and make this very simple for the less intelligent amongst us," she responded, rather sarcastically staring straight back at Freddie Fox.

"I will lead the charge with our tank division. We will crash straight through the netting creating a huge hole that our parakeet army, led by their trusty leader La Manga Lola, can get through. She will direct various low-flying squadrons all over the range floor, sending messages as they go to all the golf balls that we come in peace and ask if they have seen Putty. Freddie you can follow behind my tank and once inside go to open the doors by the barranca so that any balls that want to make a run for it, can. There's bad weather coming. They can simply roll down into the barranca and float away on the stormwater." Nel looked up thoughtfully at the ever-darkening sky as Freddie listened intently to her.

"I have a question," said Freddie, "Your plan sounds perfect apart from firstly, we don't have a tank, and secondly, I don't know where or how to open the gate."

"Oh yes, we do have a tank, Jolly Trolley! He is an old soldier of many battles and incredibly strong, running off his electric batteries. He will easily smash through the netting and fences and I shall be at his controls leading the charge. Phoebe will follow behind with Jonty, and once Lola and her parakeet army are through the gap in the fence, they will help you open the gates to the barranca. You are familiar with all the switches now after your lesson. Once we find Putty, we can carry her out in Jolly Trolley's pocket, then we can all go home."

"You are a genius Nel," said a relieved and proud Freddie Fox as he looked on at his French friend. "Never will so many owe so little to so few," he said feeling quite Churchillian. "We must get back and brief Jolly Trolley and Phoebe as we have no time to waste if we are to complete this under the cover of darkness and as the great storm breaks. The storm will create several small rivers from the range to the barranca and millions of balls will be carried to freedom on the stormwater and onto their next adventures. Let's hope that Jolly Trolley is up for this, come on let's get back to the villa, we have no time to waste."

Back at the villa, everything was quiet, as both Grandma and Grandpa were snoozing by the pool in the evening sun, and Phoebe and Jonty were playing cards in the upstairs lounge. Freddie, Nel, and Lola entered the villa through the open window of the downstairs bedroom and made their way upstairs to the buggy store for a vital meeting with Jolly Trolley.

Phoebe heard what sounded like a small army suddenly stamping to attention. She and Jonty ran to the buggy store just in time to see Jolly Trolley standing to attention and saluting Nel. "It will be a privilege to have a member of the Foreign Legion leading me into battle. I am fully charged and waiting for your command Sir, or should I say, Madame," said Jolly Trolley.

Jonty looked very confused, but Phoebe reassured him explaining that these were all her animal and thingy friends, and they were all here because they had come, after being shrunk in Grandpa's Shrinkability Cupboard, to rescue Slice's sister Putty, a golf ball!

As he wandered home Jonty felt quite dizzy and thought perhaps, he has had too much sun and needed a lie-down. Surely, he must be dreaming. I mean who has ever heard of a talking golf trolley having a conversation with a squirrel and a fox that was understood by a small girl, and what on earth was a Shrinkability Cupboard?

"When the moon has risen to the top of the tree on the far side of the barranca we should all meet and be ready to go under the cloud cover. Phoebe, you will need to bring Jolly Trolley to the edge of the barranca, where Nel will take command. Don't be late!" said Freddie Fox, very much back in control and issuing instructions clearly. In the distance, he could see the thunder clouds and the first flashes of lightning gathering over the top of the driving range. This was nothing like the Enchanted Wood and the wonderful golf course he called home, but he was confident that, if everything went well, everyone including Putty, would be on their way home the day after Grandpa's birthday.

Grandpa and Grandma felt it was time to come in, as it had become a little cooler by the pool and Grandma had decided that she would save squeezing into her new swimming costume, as a part of her special treat for Grandpa's birthday. She had knitted it especially and had followed a pattern, well nearly, that created alternative black and yellow hoops that would make her resemble a huge drowning bumblebee if she ever did actually go for the promised plunge!

Phoebe watched the moon rising. It was almost time to get Jolly Trolley out of the villa and ready for battle. As luck would have it, Grandma had decided it was shower time, and everyone needed to be ready to meet upstairs in an hour.

"Perfect timing for us," Phoebe said to Jolly Trolley, who was fully charged and raring to go. There was a little bit of clanging and banging as Jolly Trolley marched down the stairs and out of Phoebe's bedroom, across the terrace, and into the barranca. Any noise made by Jolly Trolley was drowned out by Grandma's awful tuneless singing coming from the shower.

Phoebe and Jolly Trolley were joined by Freddie Fox and Nel, who immediately jumped up onto Jolly Trolley taking over the controls from Phoebe." This is a dangerous work and too risky for a small girl," cried Nel pulling down her beret, "all stand at least a few metres behind me until we are through the electric fence and netting."

Freddie Fox gave his final instructions to Lola. "Please have all your troops ready to fly through the hole and start the search just as soon as we are inside. Phoebe don't forget we need you to open the doors into the barranca as soon as you can" Just then Phoebe saw Jonty running across the golf course, his blond hair glinting in the moonlight and his jacket flapping behind him.

"I saw you all leaving, and I thought you might need some help once you're inside," he said.

"That's fantastic news, thanks Jonty," said Phoebe as the skies went completely black. There was a lot of loud squawking as Lola and all her army landed on the surrounding trees, awaiting the instruction to enter through the soon to appear hole. The atmosphere was eerie, and everyone was incredibly nervous as the reality and enormity of the task ahead of them came home to roost, (quite literally in the case of the parakeets!)

It had just started to rain heavily when Nel shouted "Charge" and turned the dial on Jolly Trolley to full power! With a surprising turn of speed, Jolly Trolley headed straight for the fence shouting "Tally ho, keep your head down Nel some sparks are going to fly" and with an extra surge from every bit of power he could muster, Jolly Trolley charged at the fence with all the club thingamajigs sticking out in front like a battering ram.

Boom, bang, crash, wallop "Long live the Resistance," cried Nel as Jolly Trolley and she crashed through the fence leaving a huge hole for Lola and her parakeet army to fly through, a squadron at a time, peeling off in different directions flying at speed, swooping low to the ground, and calling Putty's name as they went.

Phoebe and Jonty headed up the rear, carefully avoiding the flashing wires, running as fast as they could to the garage doors that opened onto the barranca. The rain was now heavy, and the thunder and lightning very noisy, but it all created a perfect cover as the parakeets continued their search for Putty.

The rainwater was starting to form small rivers and many golf balls were on the move. The first had already rolled past Jonty and Phoebe and into the liberation of the barranca as it swept them down to the town and onwards to the coast and freedom.

"Are you looking for me?" asked a golf ball with a very muddy face but a quite unmistakable number three shaped nose. "We certainly are," said Lola, "we have come to get you out of here, now!" She let out a mighty squawk that brought Freddie Fox bounding over to where Putty was laying.

"I'm afraid we have no time for introductions," said Freddie, "we need to get you out of here quickly." In a shake of a tail Nel appeared and gathered Putty up, pushing her into her very large cheeks as if she was a precious nut, and then she scampered back to Jolly Trolley and the safety of the pockets. "Sound the retreat," cried Nel as she swung the Jolly Trolley into reverse. Nothing happened. Jolly Trolley was wounded, and his wheels refused to turn.

"Leave me and save yourself Nel, my work here is done," he said in a dying voice. "I am proud to have served." Just then Jonty and Phoebe appeared running back across the driving range jumping over thousands of golf balls, who were all rolling and marching through the newly created rivers ever closer to the barranca and freedom.

"His circuits have been shorted, we need to get him back and dry him out, he will be fine. Quick push," cried Jonty. Phoebe was already pushing as she saw the wheels start to roll forward, just before she lost her balance and fell forward with a great splat into a pile of mud face first, much to Jonty's amusement!

In no time at all everyone was back at the villa and Phoebe and Jonty had already jumped into their respective showers, but not before Phoebe had presented a very exciting Slice to his long-lost sister Putty. As they rolled together, on the duvet, it looked to the assembled crowd that they were cuddling, jumping up and down, and giving each other belly bumps in a state of pure joy at being back together.

Chapter 13
Grandpa's Birthday Round

Phoebe woke up early, very excited because today was Grandpa's birthday and she knew that she was going to play a round of golf with him and Grandma, but this time Grandma would not be a golf ball!

The sun was shining brightly, and all signs of yesterday's storm had disappeared, it was looking like it would be just perfect. Phoebe was practicing playing Happy Birthday on her saxophone, whilst enjoying the sunshine sat by the edge of the pool, for what she was certain was the start of a long party.

"Good morning," said Freddie Fox as he crawled out of the barranca with Nel the Squirrel, "What a successful day we all had," beamed Nel. "The barranca is full of even more golf balls this morning. The remote-controlled tractor continued to gather them up but missed every time he tipped them into the basket, and they just bounced off and away down the slope to freedom."

"Oh, that's even better,", cried Phoebe, "but today's Grandpa's birthday. I'm going to make him a cup of tea in bed and give him my surprise present."

"How are Slice and Putty this morning?" asked Nel, "and what about Tank Commander Jolly Trolley, how are his circuits this morning? Those was some of the bravest actions I have ever seen. I noticed that he sustained some battle scars, so I think you quickly need to check him out, especially if he is going to play golf with everyone today. He will be exhausted!"

Freddie Fox interjected, "he will also need cleaning up as the last time I saw him he was rather muddy. Please remember that we are scheduled to leave on Baggage Air first thing in the morning and you need to play your saxophone in reverse to shrink us back down to fit into Jolly Trolley's pocket for the journey home. Let's not leave that to the last minute, as we all know that this is the first time this will ever have been done and we really don't want any accidents do we Nel?"

Freddie looked up as he heard the sudden flapping of wings and the happy squawks of parakeets approaching.

"Buenos Dias, oops sorry Good morning," said Lola. "Myself and a few of the chaps flew down the length of the barranca this morning and I am pleased to report that all the escapee balls are making excellent progress and are all in great spirits. The wild boars have even been helping many balls by dropping them onto the course, so they can be claimed by the early morning golfers."

"That's great news Lola, please pass on our thanks to your flying army. We could not have done it without them," said Freddie Fox. "We could do with some extra help on the course from you today as Grandpa, Grandma and Phoebe play. I suspect they will be playing with Putty and Slice, which is great news and will be a great source of fun and happiness for all concerned, but we really can't afford to let them get lost today. We all need to be back safely in Jolly Trolley's deep pocket before the moon rises above the trees tonight."

"Leave that to me," said Lola, "I shall have eyes in the skies everywhere today and I will even speak with the wild boars to make sure they keep an eye on all the barrancas should Putty or Slice stray off course."

With a clear set of instructions and joy in her heart Phoebe was off to wrap Grandpa's present and to make him a nice cup of tea, and a slice of jam and toast for Grandma!

Grandma was already in the kitchen making Grandpa his tea and toast when Phoebe walked in. "Morning Grandma, I was just going to do that for you and Grandpa," she said.

"Oh, that's very kind darling," replied Grandma. "What a wonderful and busy day we have planned for Grandpa's birthday. We're playing golf at 11 o'clock and I've booked a nice birthday dinner for this evening. That should give us time for a swim after golf as I have a wonderful new costume I have knitted especially,", added Grandma as she gave Phoebe an excited hug and a kiss. It was then that Phoebe noticed through the buggy store that Jolly Trolley was covered in mud and looked like he had been through a battlefield, which he had. Very discretely Phoebe texted Jonty and told him to "get around here sharpish and clean everything up."

Whilst Grandpa enjoyed his birthday breakfast with Phoebe and Grandma, Jonty was busy quietly helping Freddie Fox and Nel the Squirrel, whose bushy tails came in very useful, cleaning floors and trolleys!

Grandpa was thrilled when he unwrapped his present from Phoebe, which was a wonderful new golf headcover in the shape of a fox. Grandpa commented, "It looks very similar to the one that lives by the embankment at the golf club, I love it."

"Yes, I thought that too," said a grinning Phoebe!

Grandpa was really enjoying his birthday, especially his special present of being able to play golf with his wife and wonderful granddaughter. "How lucky I am," he said on several occasions but no more so than when his ball, Slice, took a turn to the right and went into the barranca. Grandpa was certain that he had lost his ball but just then a baby wild boar, watched by her parents, ran out of the barranca and dropped Slice right next to Grandma's ball, Putty!

"Blood and stomach pills," said Grandpa, I have never seen anything like that happen before in all my years of playing golf," he said apologising for cursing as he tried to avoid Grandma's playful clip around the ear with a "Gooordon!" Phoebe saluted Lola as she flew past knowing that she and all her friends were making sure nothing happened to Putty or Slice.

"Jolly Trolley was a little slow today," said Grandma." Perhaps it's time you got a new one. I could buy you one for your birthday and we could leave the old one here" Grandma suggested.

"Not on your Nelly," said Grandpa, "today's the best game of golf I've ever had, and besides, he's like an old friend" as he turned and winked at Phoebe who was sure that Grandpa knew a lot more than he let on!

"Well in that case," said Grandma, ""I will go and get into my new costume, and we can all go for a birthday swim!"

Phoebe and Grandpa tittered to each other at the appearance of the swimming bumblebee, that Grandma resembled, as they all swam in the wonderful cool waters watched discretely by a fox, a squirrel, a parakeet, and a small boy next door.

Just before dinner Phoebe opened her bedroom door and let in Freddie Fox and Nel the Squirrel who quickly jumped onto the bed with Putty and Slice.

"It's time," said Freddie and, with that, Phoebe concentrated hard and played Three Blind Mice backwards which was not easy at all, but was the molecular deconstruction required to shrink Freddie and Nel without the need for the Shrinkability Cupboard.

"Night, night, sleep tight my little friends, we have a long journey home tomorrow," whispered Phoebe, as she placed Putty, Slice, Freddie, and Nel inside the deep pocket of Jolly Trolley, who was looking much more like his old self with a fresh charge running through his circuits.

Chapter 14
The Wanderer Returns

Everyone slept on the journey home, but they were all quite rudely awakened when the Baggage Air flight touched down with a bump in Manchester.

Grandma had some difficulty getting through customs as the young man behind the counter was rather unsure it was her, as she showed him her passport photograph. He claimed that she looked much younger in real life and that she must be Grandpa's daughter, not his wife. "That holiday has taken years off me Gordon, we should do it more often, shouldn't we Phoebe?" she said as they all made their way to the carousel to reclaim their luggage.

The screen displayed the various flight details from where each set of luggage could be claimed. The airport was very busy as several flights and luggage seemed to have arrived at once. A huge jumbo jet had just landed from Florida and was taking up several carousels with large bags and various size Mickey and Minnie Mouse's scattered in between lots of golf bags. Grandpa noticed that the Baggage Air flight was also sharing a carousel with the Florida flight as he spotted Jolly Trolley sandwiched between a Minnie and a Mickey. Phoebe stepped forward to lift him clear when a golf ball that had clearly fallen out of another bag dropped onto her foot and rolled to a stop by the side of her bag. A nice lady with an American accent said, "Oh dear it looks like someone has lost a golf ball" as she picked it up and handed it to Phoebe. Phoebe smiled as she knew it was just another lost ball with a mind of its own starting a new adventure. She looked closer and noticed a very distinctive number 1 nose.

"Quickly put me in the Jolly Trolley pocket. I am here to surprise my brother and sister; I'm Hook back from Florida."

Epilogue

Phoebe was delighted to be home and after seeing all her friends safely back to normal size and returned to the Enchanted Woods. Phoebe then found out some more exciting news that she was soon going to have a new baby sister, who would be called Erin. Hare Henry was right after all!

The End